# LOUSY ROTTEN STINKIN' GRAPES

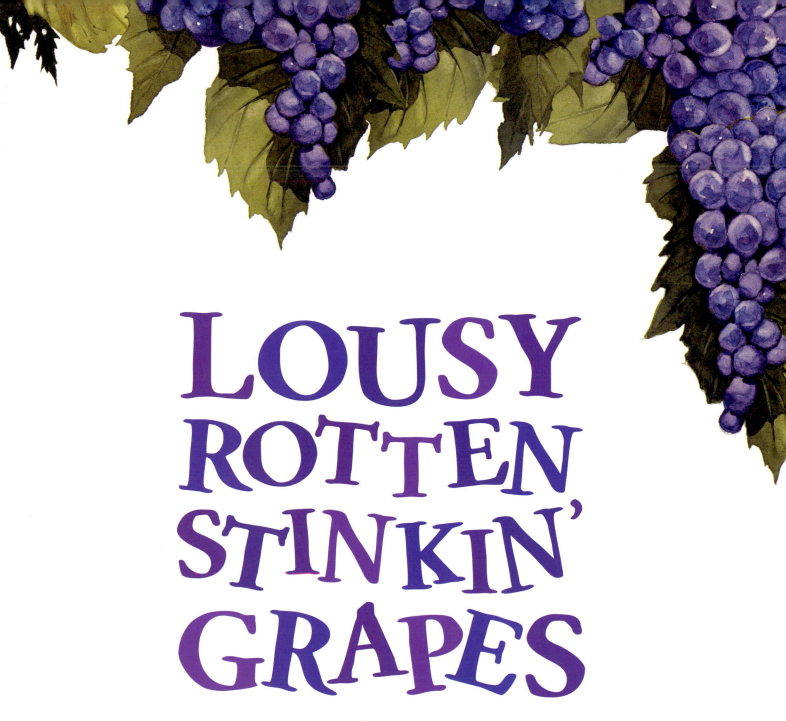

# LOUSY ROTTEN STINKIN' GRAPES

By Margie Palatini  Illustrated by Barry Moser

SIMON & SCHUSTER BOOKS FOR YOUNG READERS

*New York London Toronto Sydney*

*For Mom and Teresa and the grapes that go "pop"*—M. P.

*For my old friend, and fellow Bear, Monty Beekman.*
*Ursus Agonistes, bro*—B. M.

ACKNOWLEDGMENTS

The illustrator would like to thank Dan Harper for his very
helpful input for the fox's diagrams and plans.

SIMON & SCHUSTER BOOKS FOR YOUNG READERS
An imprint of Simon & Schuster Children's Publishing Division
1230 Avenue of the Americas, New York, New York 10020
Text copyright © 2009 by Margie Palatini
Illustrations copyright © 2009 by Barry Moser
SIMON & SCHUSTER BOOKS FOR YOUNG READERS is a trademark of Simon & Schuster, Inc.
Book design by Chloë Foglia
The text for this book is set in Revival.
The illustrations for this book are rendered in transparent
watercolor on mould-made Fabriano Artistico.
Manufactured in China
2 4 6 8 10 9 7 5 3
Library of Congress Cataloging-in-Publication Data
Palatini, Margie.
Lousy rotten stinkin' grapes / Margie Palatini ; illustrated by Barry
Moser—1st ed.
p. cm.
Summary: Retells the fable of a frustrated fox that, after many tries
to reach a high bunch of grapes, decides they must be sour anyway.
ISBN: 978-0-689-80246-1
[1. Folklore. 2. Fables.] I. Moser, Barry, ill. II. Aesop. III. Title.
PZ8.2.P25Lo 2009
398.2—dc22
[E]
2007015727

# Fox

EYED A BUNCH OF TANTALIZING GRAPES hanging from a vine growing high on a tree.

"Those juicy morsels are for me," he said with a grin.

The problem was, Fox was only so high . . . and the grapes were so, so, so high.

"No matter," said he. "I am sly. Clever. Smart. After all, I am a fox."

He made a plan.

"Add this to that. Multiply that to this. Subtract here from there, carry the two, minus the one—and *voila!* . . . Grapes!"

Hop. Skip. Jump. Flying leap. And . . .

No grapes.
Fox climbed out from the thicket and brushed off his coat.
"Perhaps a bit of a boost is needed."
But where to get a boost?

GRUNT. GRUNT. GRUNT.

Fox turned.
He grinned.
"Why, *Bear*, old buddy! I say . . . do you like grapes?"
"Grapes?" said Bear. "Uh . . . duh . . . do I? . . . I think I do. I think I do . . . Yup . . . I do."

"Excellent! Look and listen. Here's the plan," explained Fox. "You stand—here. I will stand on your head—there. On the count of three—you give a bit of a boost—and *voila!* Grapes!"

Bear looked at the plan. He looked at the grapes. He looked at the tree.

He stared at his big front paws and thought.

"Uh, duh . . . you know there, Fox . . . I'm thinkin' maybe I could just wrap my paws—"

"Ta-ta-ta-ta-ta," interrupted Fox. "Bear, Bear, Bear, my dear dim buddy. Your job is brawn. Not brain. You leave the thinking to me. After all, I'm the fox. Sly. Clever. Smart. I know how to get grapes."

Bear shrugged. "If you say so."

Bear stood here. Fox climbed up and stood on top of Bear's head—there.

Fox counted.

"One. Two. Three—and . . ."

No grapes.

Fox brushed off his coat and straightened his nose.

"Maybe a little more lift, thrust, and . . . oomph is needed here."

Bear shrugged. "If you say so."

Now, where to find oomph?

PAT. SLAP. PAT. SLAP. PAT. SLAP.

Fox peered down at the pond.

He grinned.

"Why, *Beaver*, dear pal, I say, do you like grapes?"

"Grapes?" said Beaver. "Oh, yes indeedy. Indeedy I do!"

"Excellent. Look and listen. Here's the plan," explained Fox. "Bear stands—here. You stand on Bear's head—there. I stand on your tail. And on the count of three—Bear gives a boost—as you give an oomph—which brings me—there—and *voila!* Grapes!"

Beaver looked at the plan. He looked at the grapes. He looked at the tree.

He tapped his front tooth and thought.

"Fox, I'm thinkin' if I just start a chewin' on that tr—"

"Ta-ta-ta-ta-ta," interrupted Fox. "Beaver, Beaver, Beaver, my dentally challenged chum. You just mind the oomphing. Leave all that thinking to me. After all, I'm the fox. Sly. Clever. Smart. I know how to get grapes."

Beaver shrugged. "If you say so."

Bear stood—here. Beaver stood on Bear's head—there. Fox stood on Beaver's tail.

"One. Two. Three—and . . ."

No grapes.

Fox climbed out of the brambles. "Just need an inch or two more—scooch!"

Fox measured this. He weighed that. He turned around . . . and grinned.

"Why, *Porcupine*, you short scooch of a fellow . . . do you like grapes?"

"Grapes?" said Porcupine. "I suppose I do enjoy a grape or two now and then."

"Excellent. Look and listen. Here's the plan," explained Fox. "Bear stands—here. Beaver stands—there. You stand on Beaver's tail. I stand on you. And on the count of three—Bear boosts as Beaver oomphs, while you scooch, which brings me—there—and *voila!* Grapes!"

Porcupine looked at the plan. He looked up at the grapes. He looked at his back full of quills.

"Excuse me, Fox. But I have a suggestion. Perhaps if I just point my qui—"

"Ta-ta-ta-ta-ta," interrupted Fox. "Porcupine, my little friend, let us not get all prickly. You just be a scooch and leave the ideas to me. After all, I'm the fox. Sly. Clever. Smart. I know how to get grapes."

Porcupine shrugged. "If you say so."

Bear stood—here. Beaver stood on Bear's head—there. Porcupine stood on Beaver's tail. Fox stood very carefully on Porcupine's back.

## "One. Two. Three—and . . ."

No grapes.

Fox rubbed his feet. He pulled a bramble from his tail. He uncurled his whiskers.

"What might be helpful is a wee catch and swing," said Fox, with pencil and eraser. "Yes, catch and swing should definitely do it."

Beaver looked at Bear, who looked at Porcupine.

The three shrugged. "If you say so."

Fox spied two tiny eyes peeking through a
bush. "Ah! *Possum*, my dear . . . do you like
grapes?"

"Me?" whispered Possum shyly. "Why, yes. Yes, I do like grapes. Thank you for asking. I like grapes very much."

Fox grinned.

"Excellent. Look and listen. Here's the plan. Bear stands—here. Beaver stands on Bear's head—there. Porcupine stands on Beaver's tail. I stand on Porcupine. You stand on me. So on, so on, and so on. Etcetera, etcetera, etcetera. Which lifts you—whose tail curls around here—then swings back to me—who I grab, ending up there and—*voila!* Grapes!"

Possum stared at the grapes. She stared at the branch. She stared at the plan.

"Pardon me," said Possum. "But it all seems so confusing and complicated. Perhaps if I—"

"Ta-ta-ta-ta-ta," interrupted Fox. "Possum, Possum, Possum, my pet. Now, don't worry those few little hairs on your extremely unattractive head. Nothing to fret over and faint dead away. Trust me, my dear. After all, I am the fox. I am the one here who is sly, clever, and smart. I know how to get grapes."

Possum blinked. "If you say so."

So . . .

Bear stood—here. Beaver stood—there. Porcupine stood on Beaver's tail. Fox stood—carefully—on Porcupine. And Possum stood on Fox, ready to swing into action.

"One. Two. Three—and . . ."

BOOST. OOMPH. SCOOCH. SWING.

No grapes.

"Whatcha doing?" asked Skunk.

"Blast that bunch of fruit," groused Fox, crawling out from under. "There is simply no possible way to get those grapes, and that is that!"

Possum looked at Porcupine, who looked at Beaver, who looked at Bear.

"I can run up the tree and toss them down," said Possum.

"I can aim and shoot them down," said Porcupine.

"I can cut them down," said Beaver.

"Uh . . . duh . . . I can give the tree a shake," said Bear.

Fox glared. "Oh, really? . . . Then why didn't one of you say something before?"

"Well," Possum spoke up. "After all, you are the fox."

"Sly," said Porcupine.

"Clever," said Beaver.

"Smart," said Bear. "Duh. . . . Very smart."

Fox turned with a huff and a sniff.

"Well, do as you wish. I, for one, wouldn't think of eating those lousy, rotten, stinkin' grapes now, even if I could. . . . They're probably sour anyway."

"If you say so."